Short Tales
NATIVE AMERICAN MYTHS

HOW THE WORLD WAS MADE

A CHEROKEE CREATION MYTH

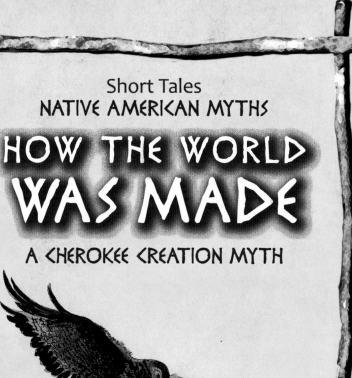

Adapted by Anita Yasuda
Illustrated by Mark Pennington

magic
wagon

visit us at www.abdopublishing.com

Published by Magic Wagon, a division of the ABDO Group, PO Box 398166, Minneapolis, MN 55439. Copyright © 2013 by Abdo Consulting Group, Inc. International copyrights reserved in all countries. All rights reserved. No part of this book may be reproduced in any form without written permission from the publisher.

Short Tales™ is a trademark and logo of Magic Wagon.

Printed in the United States of America, North Mankato, Minnesota.
052012
092012

Adapted text by Anita Yasuda
Illustrations by Mark Pennington
Edited by Rebecca Felix
Series design by Craig Hinton

Design elements: Diana Walters/iStockphoto

Library of Congress Cataloging-in-Publication Data
Yasuda, Anita.
  How the world was made : a Cherokee creation myth / by Anita Yasuda ; illustrated by Mark Pennington.
     p. cm. -- (Short tales Native American myths)
  ISBN 978-1-61641-881-6
1. Cherokee Indians--Folklore. 2. Cherokee mythology. I. Pennington, Mark, 1959- ill. II. Title.
  E99.C5Y38 2013
  398.2089'97--dc23
                        2012004692

MYTHICAL CHARACTERS

DAYUNI-SI
The water beetle

GREAT BUZZARD
The father of all buzzards

INTRODUCTION

This legend comes from the Cherokee people. The Cherokee originally lived in the southeastern United States. Cherokee myths and legends are an important way for customs, beliefs, and histories to be passed down through generations. These legends often explain natural events. Animals are commonly featured in Cherokee stories, as they are central to Cherokee spiritual beliefs.

How the World Was Made comes from a version by Katharine Berry Judson, who compiled several books on Native American myths and legends. This legend tells the story of how animals and insects worked together to create Earth. It also teaches that those who persevere are rewarded.

A long time ago, all the animals lived in Galun'lati. This was a special world far above the stone arch of the sky.

By and by, Galun'lati became crowded.

"We need more room!" the animals cried.

They became curious about the water beneath Galun'lati.

"What wonders lie beneath the water?" they asked one another.

"I will go and look, for I am not afraid," said Dayuni-si, the water beetle. Dayuni-si was Beaver's grandchild.

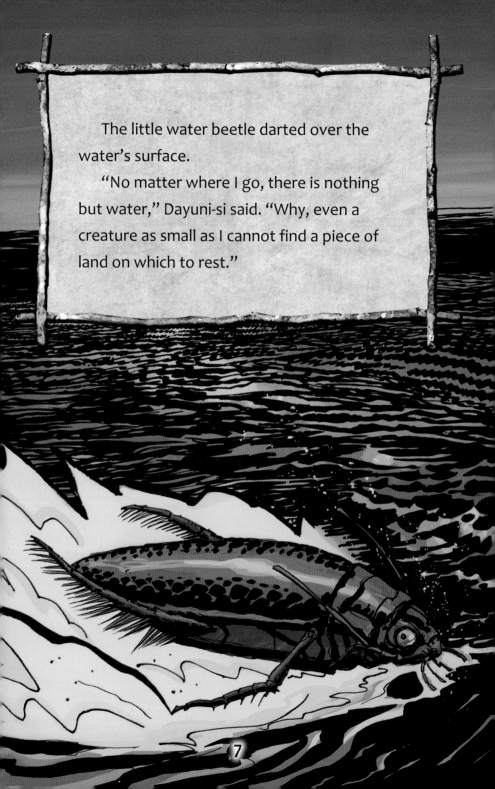

The little water beetle darted over the water's surface.

"No matter where I go, there is nothing but water," Dayuni-si said. "Why, even a creature as small as I cannot find a piece of land on which to rest."

Dayuni-si thought for a moment. "Maybe I should look beneath the water."

With that, the little water beetle dove under the water's surface. He swam deeper and deeper until he reached the mud.

"I should bring this mud up to the surface," Dayuni-si thought.

He gathered up as much mud as he could carry and swam to the surface.

The mud Dayuni-si brought to the surface began to grow and spread. The mud spread and spread, reaching in four directions.

The animals watched in amazement as the mud grew into the massive island of Earth. The island was fastened to the sky with four special cords, but no one knows by whom.

Earth was soft and flat. It was also very wet. The animals asked the birds, "Would you please fly down and see if Earth is dry enough for us to come down?"

"We will check," the birds said, and they flew down. One by one, the birds returned to Galun'lati.

"There is no place to rest on Earth," each bird said. "It is still far too wet for animals."

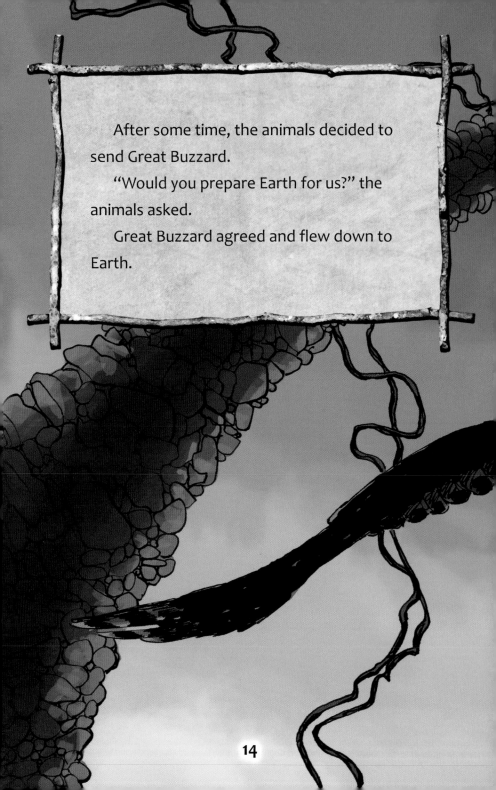

After some time, the animals decided to send Great Buzzard.

"Would you prepare Earth for us?" the animals asked.

Great Buzzard agreed and flew down to Earth.

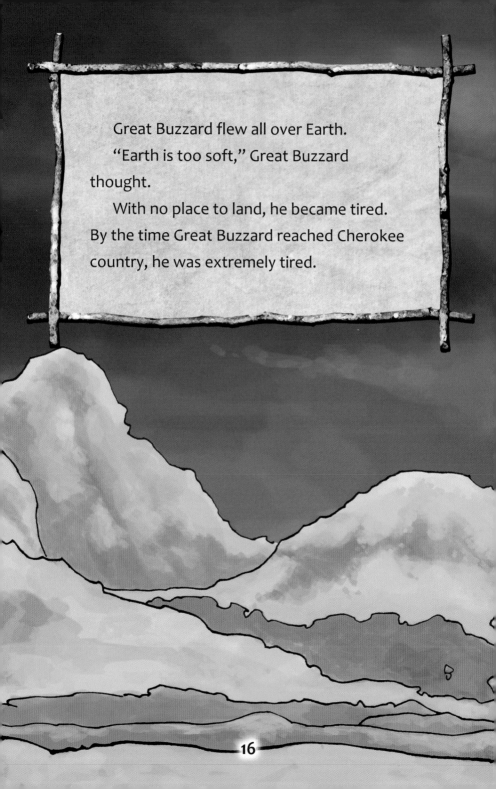

Great Buzzard flew all over Earth.

"Earth is too soft," Great Buzzard thought.

With no place to land, he became tired. By the time Great Buzzard reached Cherokee country, he was extremely tired.

"I cannot fly without hitting the ground!" he exclaimed.

Each time Great Buzzard's wings hit the ground, a valley formed. Each time he turned his wings up again to fly, a mountain formed.

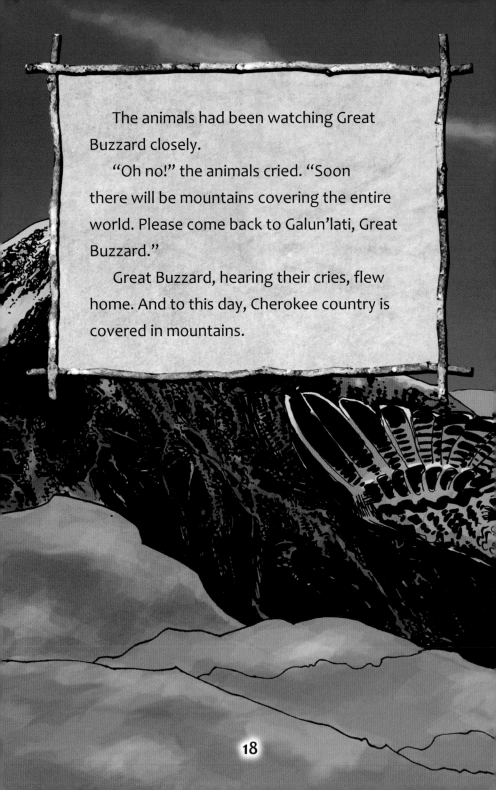

The animals had been watching Great Buzzard closely.

"Oh no!" the animals cried. "Soon there will be mountains covering the entire world. Please come back to Galun'lati, Great Buzzard."

Great Buzzard, hearing their cries, flew home. And to this day, Cherokee country is covered in mountains.

19

Earth was not finished yet. "There is only darkness," the animals said. "We must bring light to Earth."

So they got the sun and placed it on a track in the sky right above Earth. Then they traveled down to their new home.

"Look at the sun!" the animals said. "See how it travels across the island from east to west."

At first, the sun was too low. "Earth is too hot," the animals said.

"My poor shell!" the crawfish cried. "It has been scorched bright red. My meat is forever spoiled."

And from then on, the Cherokee did not eat crawfish.

Four medicine men appeared and had an idea. "We will try to raise the sun higher," they said.

They managed to raise the sun, but Earth was still too hot.

It was decided to raise the sun even higher. The medicine men pushed the sun higher until it was just under the stone arch of the sky. Earth was no longer too hot.

"Now it is just right," the animals said.

Earth's first plants and animals were then made, but no one knows by whom.

Upon creation, the plants and animals were told they must stay awake for seven days and seven nights.

"We will try," they said.

On the first night, all the animals and plants stayed awake.

On the second night, some of the animals fell asleep. On the following nights, even more animals fell asleep.

By the seventh night, only a few of the animals, including the owl and the panther, were awake.

It was decided—but no one knows by whom— that they would be rewarded. These animals were given the power to see at night.

During those seven nights, some of the trees went to sleep, too. "And that is why we shed our leaves each winter," they said.

"But we stayed awake," the cedar, pine, spruce, holly, and laurel said. These trees were allowed to always stay green.

People came after the plants and animals. In the beginning, there was only one man and one woman.

The man struck the woman with a fish. Seven days later, a child came to Earth, and another came every seven days after.

Soon, there were so many people that it was decided—but no one knows by whom—that a woman would give birth once a year. And the legend says that this is how it was to be from then on.

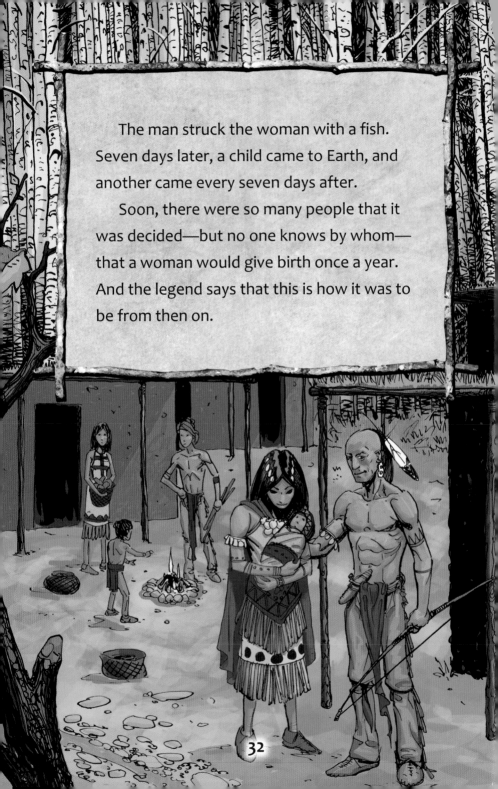